KATHERINE MYERS

Where Did We Start?

Collection of Flash-fiction

First edition

ISBN: 979-8-9920568-1-5

Cover art by Natalia Junqueira

This book was professionally typeset on Reedsy. Find out more at reedsy.com

To Grandma: LYMTATSIM

— — —

To Grandpa: Thank you for all you ever did for me.
I hope you can read this up in Heaven.

— — —

And to myself who is trying her best to follow her dreams.

Contents

Preface

This collection contains
Trigger Warnings: Mentions of blood, death, and suicide.

★: Not Grandma Approved
Note: Grandma's may vary

1

Memory Lane

What if Memory Lane was a real place? What would be there? Who would be there? What happens there? And how do you get there?

I never thought I would get any of those answers. Well, there is one I still don't know the answer to: How long is Memory Lane? I'm not sure if it ever actually ends.

Every time a memory is made, the location appears on the lane. Even if the location exists, another one appears. The who? Those who have had any impact on you.

What happens? Well, it's quite weird. No one on Memory Lane interacts with the other memory locations. They have a set location, and each day the memory is played out at the same time it happened.

How do you get to Memory Lane? Easier than I thought it would be, honestly. You see, being nostalgic doesn't bring you to Memory Lane. It may be part of it, but not all of it. Dying and having your life flash before your eyes isn't it either. You get to Memory Lane by one action: Looking for the person you have truly forgotten. Not the friend that has moved on, but the old you, the one before you grew up. The one that helped mold the you of today.

2

The Fallen

"I am no longer your servant…I will not serve you." The man knelt on the ground before the throne.

"You are my soldier. You will raise your head and take to the sky. That is an order," the King who sat upon the throne demanded.

The man's wings were soaked with blood. "I will not."

"An order was given to you, soldier. RISE!"

"No," The man said, "I will join the ranks of The Fallen before I take your orders again."

"You will do no such thing." The King drew his sword and placed it on the neck of the man before him.

"Then kill me." The man spread his wings out as his blood dripped onto the floor.

"I am your king. You obey my commands." The King pressed the sword into the neck of the man.

"I am no more than a tool to you. I obey no one. Do you understand, your majesty?" The man hissed, grabbing the sword with his bare hand. The king released the sword and stumbled back to the throne. The man dropped the sword and ran from the throne room, leaving behind a pile of blood-soaked feathers.

3

Roots

My roots twist and turn, and the magic of all runs beneath my bark. The magic that allows me to see what I could never have seen without it. They don't know that I know. They want my magic.

I have been burned. I have been stabbed. I have been robbed. They wish to take from me all that gives my home life. They care not for me, but for the magic.

The child hiding in my branches traces the bark damaged by knives and axes. I protect her. They tried to kill her, but she lived. I know she will protect me when she is big enough. They want my magic because they think that they can rule the world. If they take my magic, this place will die. I watch, the child bleeds and I lend her my magic to heal her wounds.

Together we are bound.

4

What I Remember

I remember a day when life was quiet. I remember when I would play. I remember the sun. I remember the moon. I remember the noise. I remember when I lived. I remember when I died.

The sun would rise and I would go out to play. My friends and I would play games quietly in the woods. As time went on we began to play in the dark with the moon and the clashing of the machines. Our parents didn't like our choices, but we made it clear *this was what we wanted.*

The sun had risen like it always had, the moon waiting for its time to shine. The noise of the city had long echoed in my ears. I had not returned home; I was trapped here. No one knew where I was, even now no one knows, and I am still trapped. My mother will cry and so will my father…

This isn't what I wanted.

5

Lost in the Woods

"Stay close, come on," Matthias said, pulling his sister closer.

"Where are we? How did we get here?" Fear laced his sister's voice.

"I'm not sure." Matthias looked around at the woods around them. They had woken up here and couldn't remember anything.

The trees felt like they were closing in on them. The air was becoming suffocating. The night was falling and they had nowhere to go.

"We need shelter," Rita complained, pulling her brother's arm and attention back to her.

"I know." Matthias patted her head.

"No one's looking for us are they?" Rita asked.

"We don't know how we got here. How would anyone know we were missing?"

They walked for hours after darkness had fallen and found nothing. The moonlight barely reached the ground through the branches of the trees.

"I'm tired," Rita complained, "My feet hurt." She sat on the ground next to her brother.

"I know. I am too." Matthias knelt and hugged her.

"What should we do?" She pouted up at him.

"We wait...we hope someone comes and finds us." He sighed, lying down next to his sister. She laid down beside him.

After a few minutes, a voice from the woods whispered in their ears, "Not quite..."

Rita's scream echoed in the darkness of the forest as blood ran from her brother's body beside her.

6

The White Room

Not quite nothing, but it wasn't quite something either. The room seemed to have no end, at least that could be seen. Aya had no idea how she had gotten here. The white that encased this space seemed as though it were glowing. Aya tried to call for help or an answer, but she found she had no voice. Aya became scared and began to run around the room.

She hoped that she could find some answers here. Soon she ran into something at waist level; she doubled over in pain. She placed her hands on this seemingly invisible table before her. On the table, there sat a card with bold text and it read:

Banished from existence.

Aya couldn't believe what she was reading. She couldn't find any answers as she tried to figure out what she could have done. She leapt to her feet and began to run again…There had to be a way out…Right? She ran into another table and another as she kept running.

How could she be banished from existence…what could she have done?

7

No Longer Me

"I'm no longer the little girl you left to die anymore," Lilia spoke wiping blood from her bottom lip. In her other hand, she clutched a knife. The man who stood before her just stared in silence at her.

"It—" He tried to start.

"Don't play." She laughed. "You never thought you'd see me again, did you?" She smiled lifting her eyes to watch him cower.

"I…I…"

"Blood shall bleed. It will fill their cups." She hissed under her breath as she stepped closer to him and raised her knife. "Kneel!" She commanded.

The man stood frozen in fear looking down into the eyes of the young woman.

"I said kneel," Lilia said softly, pressing the knife against the man's neck forcing him to the ground before her.

"How…" He whispered.

"They saved me. Now your blood will feed them. Just like you thought it would once be mine that did." The knife slid down along his jaw. "I won't show you mercy." She hissed in his ear, still slowly moving the knife, careful not to do more harm than intended. His blood ran down his neck and dripped onto the floor.

8

Missing

My sister's notebook sits on her desk. Last Sunday she demanded that no one touch it. It's been a week, and curiosity makes me need answers. On Monday she ran a marathon, and on Tuesday she disappeared. Everyone thinks she is dead, but I don't know what to think.

She loved the beach; our walls were covered in posters of islands all over the world. I know she loves the waves of the sea as much as I love the stars.

She is gone. She kept her secret, but I can't wait. I need answers. I hope she'll understand.

I pick up the notebook and open it. I am met with my sister's beautiful handwriting: *Good luck out there, Sis. See you in the future.*

She is gone...but alive.
I will find her.

9

Life and Death

Once there was a beautiful girl, with makeup always caked on her face. Everyone seemed to love her, but some abused her friendship. She constantly lied to those around her, and many people would be angry at her.

There was also a boy, who was average and a loner. He was blunt but always honest, yet people hated him more than they hated the girl who lied. He was painfully aware of her presence even though she hardly seemed to know he existed.

Everyone wanted to hold her hand and walk alongside her, but no one could imagine wanting to walk alongside him. So if they were to learn that the face beneath the makeup-caked face was as saddened as the boy's, what would the world say? Would they scream and cry that it must be a lie? Or would they realize that everything isn't as *perfect* as they always think?

10

The Flowers Died on Monday

The flowers died on Monday, but they died too soon. We... I... wasn't ready to say goodbye. At least not yet. People tell me I'll always remember, but I know myself too well. Once all the connections are gone, I won't remember.

A week since I was given the flowers. One week I dreaded the final goodbye. The day the flowers would wilt. One week I did all I could to bring back what I had lost and keep my flowers alive.

I can't keep them, but I want to. They have wilted. If they stay here, they will bring bugs, and I can't have bugs.

I'll go throw them out. Why did we have to say goodbye? Why could you not stay, even just a little bit longer?

A final goodbye, no way to remember you. Lost memories once time moves from now. Perhaps I'll dream of you. I hope. I want to remember you. I'll miss you as long as I remember.

Another Tuesday.

11

Dragons Must Fly

A dragon's wings are meant to carry them far across the world, but their wings are weak for some. They cannot fly as far or to where they aim to go. The winds from others rush by, a laugh, to those whose wings are weak.

A dragon plain and unnoticed. Dull, simple, and quiet, this dragon's skills remained unmatched. The dragon's fire roars unheard. Eyes that admire without words.

The others watch as the dragon reaches to fly further, other dragons who are as plain and dull as he is. The dragons who watch with admiration are waiting for his voice to tell them he'll fly. He chose his time to fly, and for that they understood. If he had to fly alone in his own winds, then that is how that dragon must fly.

For all dragons must fly.

12

Broken

She'd been cheated and lied to. She was strung along because it couldn't be fake.

She'd loved him with every piece of her heart and he didn't even care at all. His heart belonged to someone else, but SHE couldn't believe who it belonged to, her best friend. The girl who cooed and aahed at all the cute stories she told as her heart loved so hard. His heart was ice to a girl whose heart was one of fire.

She'd lost her heart to two different loves.

To romance.

To friendship.

She'd lost most of what she once had. Her best friend, with whom she had shared many secrets, and the man she'd loved and would have given anything for if he asked.

She'd lost herself. She no longer knew who to trust.

13

Lost & Found

"Can you hear me?" Merewin called out into the night.

No one answered. Under his feet, the grass was soft, and around him, the air was chilled.

"We have to go home!" Merewin called out again. Once more no one answered. The only sound was the winds rustling the leaves overhead. No moon or trees did shine this night.

"Then go…" A voice whispered in his ear.

"Who?" Merewin spun towards the voice. "Not without my friend."

"What if he left without you?" The voice asked.

"He wouldn't…Who are you?" Merewin asked again.

"Oh, don't worry about who I am…It doesn't matter."

"Can you help me find my friend?" Merewin whispered fear lacing his voice.

"I suppose." The voice called from somewhere further ahead of Merewin now.

"Where are we going?" Merewin asked, stumbling in the dark. He'd been walking for what seemed to be hours. The ground had changed from plush grass to sharp rocks under his feet. "I don't think he'll be up here."

"It's the only place to go…" The voice whispered in his ear.

"He wouldn't have gone this far. I'm going back…" Merewin went to turn around.

"It's just a little further." The voice called from up the hill.

"I can't see anything…I should have just gone home." Merewin forced himself to climb a little further even though he was scared.

"Yes…" The voice hissed in his ear. "You should have just gone home."

Merewin lashed out at the voice as fear once more took hold but in his panic threw himself over the edge of the cliff on which he stood.

The laugh of the voice was eerie and echoing as he fell…and fell…and fell.

14

Imaginary Friend

She's crying. I want to help, but I can't; she won't let me. She's forgetting me, and I can't make it stop. I'm fading soon and soon I'll be lost.

We used to play games, like tag and hide 'n' seek. We'd share secrets. I was a defender to protect her from the monsters in the dark. I never failed her, but I am failing her now.

I am Avi the Defender! She is Iva, my person.

Iva thought me into existence. I have ears like a teddy bear and am strong like a lion, even if I'm small.

I'm still small, and she has grown big. It's too late. She has to fight her own monsters now.

I wish I could help, just one last time.

15

Other World

Let me tell you of my world.

Grass that is soft and plush, a beautiful blush. Trees with leaves of purples and blues, that grace the tops of these yellow and orange trunks. The sky is pale green. Water rushes red down the rivers, as the liquid pours from the lakes of a much deeper red. Flowers of greens of all types, the lights, the darks, the flowers bloom bright.

This is my world, one I view every day with wonder. The beauty seems so surreal some days, even to me.

This is my world.

16

The Book on the Train

He found the notebook on the train. It was compressed between the seats. He didn't read it all only a page or two. The pages were yellowed from time. Whoever this book belonged to had left it here long ago. If the owner had left a name it had faded, much like the title on the front. The book's binding was not in disrepair.

When he pulled it from the crevice, he flipped through it once. The title read, *Warning for the Future.* The words flashed by as he thumbed quickly through, and at the end caught sight of the words, *I have warned you.* He placed the book back to where he'd found it. He wasn't sure what to do, he didn't want to know what this book was about.

A few weeks later, the news reported a train crash, and in the remains, they found a journal that told the story of a train that would be wrecked because the cursed man had read the book. The man hadn't told a soul about that book, and he hadn't stepped foot on that train again—*at least until he did.*

17

Peace of Rain

The rain was pouring down in sheets. There was bellowing thunder and lightning as the sea raged against the rocks by the lighthouse. The lighthouse beam pierced the depth of the night.

Here in the park from where the sea could be seen, a young lady sat watching the light as it searched. From head to toe, she was soaked, but she didn't seem to mind. As others rushed by, not caring for the weather that poured down around them, she sat on a bench. Her nose was red and runny from the cold of the rain, but she showed no hurry to get out of the rain. Thunder seemed to shake the sky, but she seemed to not notice.

Out in the sea highlighted between flashes of lightning, a boat was suffering from the waves. This boat was beautiful from where she sat, a small beast fighting against an unbreakable foe. The waves would rattle those who stood upon that ship, but if the storm could pass they would find peace. For this young lady though, peace came with the rain, not after.

A storm could not cause her to be fearful and faint but kept her heart light.

18

On the Cliff

A figure stood on the edge of the cliff. The breeze swept the cloak, which was ragged from time. The person stared out at the ocean. The sun had long set from the sky, and now only the stars and moon gave light in this place.

Solemn, quiet, serene.

The wind, the ruffling of the cloak, and the crashing waves below. Somewhere in the distance, boat horns sounded and machines clamored.

The figure remained still, the hood fluttered but didn't fall. Without a word, the figure stepped forward and plummeted to the ocean below.

The sounds didn't change as the ocean swallowed the figure. In the distance, the machines continued to clamor.

19

Marked

When I was born, mom and dad both thought my mark was an eight. The doctors and nurses thought so too. Why would it be something else?

The reason they found it was not, was after they left the hospital. My 'eight' didn't look like other eights. The marks all have the same font, so mine was different. No one knew what it meant. How could someone have lived an infinite amount of lives?

Most people get glimpses into past lives, about their fears, things they loved, and what they knew how to do. I don't. I've tried. I haven't been successful.

∞—seemingly a mark that causes me to become an outsider, a weirdo.

The infinity symbol sits placed between my shoulder blades. One of the few things that differed with marks was the placement of them. People have marks in the range of 1-1000 and sometimes even more.

I have lived ∞ lives and I do not understand.

20

Heart of Ink

The ink spills. It runs in rivers as it shapes its way across the paper. It is all unplanned, a rage-filled storm, that the bottles of ink were thrown. The colored inks mix in pools of brown and black where their colors meet.

The ink seeps deeper through the paper into the wood of the desk now unattended. This desk is the home of artworks long favored by the people of Duskworth. Duskworth's people demand that the artist make more works to furnish their homes. However, the artist has no motivation, no inspiration, and no will to please these people anymore. They, the artist, has given Duskworth everything; the people have taken the joy from the artist's work. Now the desk is soaked with ink, and the artist returns to their chair with a rope.

21

A Teardrop

She cries. Her tears are magical and promising. They sparkle as though filled with glitter. Vials of tears that sparkle no matter the lighting. Magical beyond what anyone could dream.

These tears will change the world, yet not in the way you may expect. They are tears of death, just a drop can cause the world to rot.

Soon the tears will rain from the sky. We will say goodbye to what has once been, as we welcome a new age of The Rotting, a world that wilts and cannot continue to grow. A world that's different from the one we live in now.

Don't get me wrong. I love life, but magic is far more compelling than life.

The adrenaline is ecstasy in life after all.

Doesn't magic sound compelling to you?

22

The Camera Never Lies

"The camera never lies." Grandma would always say when she took our photos.

I never saw the photos. No one did.

Grandma's gone now. Most of her belongings are now in my possession. Among them: a photo book and the camera.

The camera was old it was a miracle to me that it even still worked, but Grandma took good care of it that was for certain.

The photo book, bound by leather, is the place where she told us she kept all the photos she took.

To relive some memories I open the book, greeted by a face that I know, but the photo is so old. I know she wasn't that old back then. In the next photo, two men and a woman, my brother and sister. My brother looks no older than the day he died. My sister and I are older than we are now, but how? The photo is from my tenth birthday. There is a note from Grandma: *Life is beautiful, see you on the other side.*

23

The Sea

I love the sounds of cracking wood, and these days the splitting sound from metal, each has such a satisfying breaking sound.

It's so much harder these days. Metal takes a lot more power to break. The ships used to be so easy to sink. In the past, I would sink ships in my free time. I still do, but I don't get to do it as often.

Damage is one thing, but they, the land creatures, have perfected it as well as they can, the *structure*. But no matter if I sink them, they are at MY mercy. They cannot control me and they never will.

I as an entity am immovable. Damaged perhaps, but not down for the count.

I will drown them, and then the ships will sink once more.

24

After Death

"Hell isn't a place." Death explained.

"Then what is it?" The person beside Death asked.

"A state of mind." Death answered, turning to walk away.

"No, that can't be right." The person shook their head.

"Why can't it be? Millions of people have died, so tell me; why Hell isn't just a state of mind?" Death asked with a sigh.

"A state of mind is not a physical place. Hell has to exist otherwise-"

"No. Hell is the feeling of regretting how you lived your life. Or the regret is forced onto you by the Entities of the After." Death spoke, irritation lacing his voice.

"The Entities? As in God and the Devil?"

"If you believe in that, yes. I am also an Entity of the After."

"So the After is a place?" The person asked confused.

"Yes. The After is a place, and I have done my duty as the transport Entity. So if the Twins would arrive so I may take my leave that would be fantastic. I must get going." Death turned to walk away again, as two more Entities appeared.

25

A Dragon Vet

"'Be a veterinarian for dragons' they said. 'It'll be fun' they said. Why'd I listen to the village elders?" I mumble to myself as I work, my clothes an armor made of dragon scales. Without it, I'd be crisply cooked.

Today Rougert needs a check-up; he's been munching on some castle knights as of late. He isn't trying to hurt me, but it's better safe than sorry.

While being a vet for the dragons may not be as fun as promised, I know it is important. The dragons protect us from the king and his men, so keeping them healthy is the least we can do.

Good news for the dragons, they are pretty easy to fix up as long as they aren't too injured.

As long as they help us we will help them and that is the real reason I am a dragon veterinarian.

26

Destroyed Beyond Us

"THIS IS ALL YOUR FAULT!" Aliya yelled at Levi.

"I hope so!" Levi laughed. They stood looking out over the town that was charred and flooded all at once.

"How can you say that Levi? That's our home!" Aliya grabbed Levi shaking him.

"So?" Levi asked tilting his head to the side.

"So you destroyed it. How can you destroy your home?"

"Aliya, it never was my home. The unwanted child—that's all I ever was down there." Levi pried her hands off of him.

"No, you're wrong. Levi, you were a friend and family. We loved you down there, and you destroyed it. You destroyed anything you did have because no one will forgive you for this."

"I didn't start the fire, that's on you. I caused the flood."

"Don't blame me. "

"You should have just let me go, Aliya. You should never have tried to stop me. I don't care that your home is gone."

"Levi! Please, everyone down there loved you. How could you hurt them like this?" Aliya reached again to grab Levi.

Levi had stepped away from her and smiled. "Goodbye, Aliya.

I'll go rejoin the ocean now." He turned on his heel and headed down to the flooded town.

27

Only I

There used to be six of us, but now I am alone. Why did only I make it?

Brighton, Ember, Gale, Amon, and Avis. I'll never forget them and they will always haunt me.

When water runs it's darkened route of the river, I'll hear as Amon cries out for our help. He was whisked away out of reach, out of sight, but we could hear him still, until he stopped. Avis and Gale walked too close to the edge, and because the wind had been strong that day, they fell. Their screams were eerie as they echoed.

Brighton, Ember, and I continued with heavy hearts. Brighton soon fell ill with a cold that he just couldn't seem to shake. Ember and I did what we could, but gained oh so little. He passed peacefully at least…more than the others.

Through time Ember had gone crazy. They lost who they were and just wanted out. I tried to help; and give hope, but I was no help. The fire started and I ran. Even though I could hear Ember's screams, I couldn't help.

I am Rosemary.

WHERE DID WE START?

I wish I couldn't remember.

28

I Tried

We had known each other for years. We played games and laughed as the years passed. We continued to be happy until one day, she glanced down at her phone. In that moment I saw the life leave her eyes, even if she wasn't dead. I wanted to ask, but she didn't speak. The smile she wore for the rest of the day was painfully fake, it broke my heart.

She never told me what it was, but I did what I could to try and bring the life back to her eyes.

The spark was gone, and it wouldn't come back. Her laughs were hollow and the smiles fake. Her words lies from space that I could not reach. I wanted to help her but she wouldn't accept my hand.

I decided to let her go.

I'm sorry.

I tried.

29

A Bubble of Glass

We live in a glass bubble. The world is too polluted outside. The filtered air is how we must survive. That's what we are told.

The small space we have that is considered a yard touches; the dome, luckily, it is hidden from sight. A few days ago a hand-print had appeared dusty and on the other side of the glass. I didn't see anyone, but even if I had, it would have been impossible. More hand-prints appear day by day, all the same shape and size.

Every day I try to get out and see who it is, but every day they are gone. Until today I reached the glass dome, and a boy stood on the other side. As soon as he saw me he vanished. I walked over and spent all day looking out of the glass. The next morning the same thing happened.

One day when I sat in front of the glass there were no hand-prints. I reached out and placed my hand on the glass. After nearly an hour like this, a dusty hand-print appeared, and with it the boy.

The boy watched me as he slowly wrote on the glass with dirt:

I am lonely.

30

It's a Lie

The number on my wrist has always stared back at me sadly whenever I look at it.

I watch as children run about full of talk of popularity throughout their lives. To be honest with you, at that age I'd agree that that's what the numbers meant. Most would be average, some special, and others as popularity goes "losers", but I have grown and learned. My confirmation was three years ago, at the funeral of my best friend. Her number was six. Myself, her daughter and daughter's husband, as well as her son and her two grandchildren were the only ones there.

I know who will be at my funeral. I never married or had children, but I have a caretaker, and the *one* on my wrist, no matter what it means, is sad.

I will not tell what I believe to anyone. It is far sadder for a child to be faced with the fact there may not be anyone there for them at the end, or that they may leave far sooner than expected.

Sometimes a lie is the right choice.

31

Today I Summon

I am the youngest Vernitillon, the weakest summoner family in the Kollective. A summoner's familiar represents the strength they have for using their powers. Today I turn ten, the age when power manifests. My eldest brother's familiar was a rat. My other brother a songbird. My sister has a snake, but even her snake is docile.

Mom and Dad both have crows. I want to be able to prove we are capable. I am scared. I don't want to be laughed at.

"You got this." My sister whispers in my ear. Her familiar is wrapped around her wrist, it's glowing faint. Behind her, my brothers stand with their familiars perched on their shoulders.

I shake my head unsure, and she rolls her eyes in response. I walk away towards the center of the Circle of the Kollective. Before me now are the Leaders of the Kollective, the strongest of the summoners, and my parents with their familiars.

I take a deep breath and seek within to call for my familiar. Soon the feeling of finding my familiar warms my body as it releases out into the circle around me. The space has gone quiet. I am too nervous to open my eyes, but I know I must.

I open my eyes and find myself nose-to-nose with a wolf— a wolf whose coat glows brightly. I reach out and touch its head.

I will prove what we the Verntillion can do.

32

"It's Not Safe!"

"Don't! It's not safe! You'll die!" Lina snapped, grabbing the younger man's arm.

"I can make my own choices, Lina." Alec shook his arm from his friend's grasp.

"Do you not understand what she's trying to say?" The other woman asked. She knelt holding two small children close to her.

"I do. If I do this I die, but we will all die if I don't, Tilly. I know what I'm doing. Okay? I'd do it in every life if it means you'll all live." Alec smiled at both the women and the two children. "So, GO! NOW!" Alec ran off, and the creatures that were hunting took off after him, they were fast.

"Go…" The children whispered. They took off in the other direction.

"Al-" Lina started to call.

"Shh." Tilly hissed back, following after the children.

"But…" Lina whispered.

"You heard him. He knew what he was doing. He said he'd do it again. Don't let it be for nothing. We have to go before they come back. Please, Lina." Tilly grabbed her hand and pulled.

33

The Signs Warn

The signs warn of danger. The mouth of the cave looms overhead. In the village, they warn *'No man has passed this point and lived'*. People still go. Thousands have gone in...no one has come out.

Some say it is a monster.

Others say it is a lost world, superior to our own, and that's why no one comes back.

Both seem like they could be true.

I'll tell the world...I hope.

They said they would come back no matter what. That was ten years ago. They haven't come home, and I am tired of waiting for them.

The cave is instantly dark as I cross the boundary. I don't know if I want to keep going, but I can't turn around. I hear noises coming from the depths.

"Come home!"

"It's fantastic!" Their voices call to me.

I follow. I stare out into the cavern before me.

I am scared...no, I am terrified.

43

WHERE DID WE START?

I should have listened.

34

We Failed Them

We buried them long ago, our friends and our families. They were buried at the top of the mountain; we built them an altar there. They were the ones who should have lived. We failed them; we were not able to protect them, and they died.

My mother once told me that the dead haunt those who failed them, in life. I know all too well that is true now; we all do. Each night we are kept awake by the cries of the dead that echo over the land. We can't face our failures, so rarely do we, the living, visit the altar.

Today we will go to the grave. It's been nearly a year since we went. My mother would have hit me if she could. Had she known I wouldn't visit the grave of everyone I ever knew, she would have threatened me with far more than a haunting. As we climb closer to the altar, the air becomes heavy and the feelings uneasy. My few remaining warriors kneel at the altar. As I kneel to join them I notice, that the grave is open and it lies empty, when once it was full. The hole is deep, and within should be bones, *but the dead have vanished.*

35

Time Moves Slow

One. The knife is drawn.

Two. The man lunges toward me, I cannot move.

Three. Silver turns red.

Four. Pain...It hurts...I bleed.

Five. I cannot stay on my feet, I fall to the ground.

Six. The world has gone hazy. I can no longer hear. The pain is less. I have lost, but what was I trying to win?

One. I'm a kid playing games.

Two. I'm a rebellious teen.

Three. I'm in love.

Four. I am broken.

Five. I am here.

Six. Time is up. No one else came. I could not be saved. *My clock ran out.*

36

All is Lost

It's gone. All of it is gone. I think as I stand at the edge of the burned village.

I walk through the rubble of the place I once called home, looking for signs of anything. Signs of life—that was all I cared to find.

The fountain in the center of the village is what brings me to tears. The water still flows; it is untouched by the destruction.

Memories of playing with my siblings and friends play in my head. The tears fall from my eyes, but I have to keep going.

I reach the house that when it stood housed my family. The tears continue to fall as I walk through the burnt house. I braced myself for the worst. I know I had lost everything, but when I reach what had been the room that they shared. I ran. I shouldn't have gone.

Two skeletons had been huddled together for safety. A new haunted memory to remember them by.

37

A Chance

"You knew, didn't you?" Vyc asked, turning to look at Brack.

"Yeah…" Brack whispered.

"Why didn't you tell me?" Vyc yelled, grabbing his friend.

"Would you have believed me?" Brack glanced up offering his hand that was glowing green to Vyc.

"I don't know," Vyc answered, holding Brack's hand, "But I should have been given the chance. I deserved that much didn't I?"

"I know… I'm sorry. Vyc, I didn't want to hurt you."

"Then why?" Vyc crushed Brack's hand in his own.

"I don't get it either…this magic…why do I have it? What do I do with it?" Brack screamed, pulling his hand away from Vyc. "You're hurting me."

The green magic swirled over Brack's fingers and up his arms while lingering softly over his scars.

"I'm sorry… we can figure this out… together, okay?" Vyc asked, reaching out for Brack. Brack nodded and hugged Vyc, allowing the magic he did not understand to wrap around them.

38

Our Future

"What's wrong with you?" Astra asked, grabbing Teo's arm.

"Forgive me." He shook her off. "You'll know soon enough."

"Just tell me, Teo! Don't keep secrets from me!"

"I know…" Teo looked at the ground

"What is going on?" Astra yelled, grabbing Teo again.

"Please forgive me…Astra?"

"For what? You haven't done anything."

"I promised you, we'd see the world just like everyone else."

"And we will. Teo? We will see the world just like all of them, way up there, and then we'll start a life just like they all have." Astra smiled up at him.

"We won't." Teo shook his head.

"Why not?" Astra frowned.

"You will." Teo pushed Astra into the last life pod and latched it.

"No! Not without you! Please Teo? Don't do this."

"I love you, Astra. Enjoy the stars for me?"

Before Astra could answer, Teo pressed the force launch button outside of the pod.

39

My Reflection

I stare into the mirror. The person that's there is...is...is me, I guess. I turn and walk away.

Then once more I turn to look. I can't look for too long. I fear I'll get lost.

I go about my day, and once again, when I get home, I walk past the mirror.

I hear words whispered. *"Just look at me."*

I turn to face myself in the shattered mirror. My reflection is misshapen as the fractures run throughout the mirror, and some pieces lay on the floor. I'm tired of looking but I can't seem to turn away.

In the mirror, the blackened veins that run like tendrils across my body seem more prevalent than ever.

I finally pull away. I cannot let myself get lost, my reflection will consume me.

Some days my reflection seems to be someone else, but inside I know that *we are the same.*

40

In the Boat

"Hello!" The little girl yells, leaping into my boat.

I stare at her confused. No one else came with her.

"I chose to come here!" She starts seeming to sense my confusion. "By myself, well no. I didn't choose. I just got here. You seem nice, so I chose to see where your boat was going."

Not many people willingly choose my company.

"Can you not talk?" She asks, leaning towards me.

I shake my head.

"Oh…Well, in that case, I'm Sammy. I was really sick, but I feel much better now. Are you the Grim Reaper?"

Once I would have nodded, but once I would have also shaken my head too. I shrug.

Sammy seems to study me before grabbing my hand softly. "Are you my guide to the next world? Mom and Dad called it Heaven."

If I could smile, I would have, as I nodded and picked up my oars and we headed out on the water.

41

The Sky is Dark

The ship must be massive, as it is miles overhead and yet takes up so much of the sky.

No one has seen any of the beings, but we know there must be thousands, or they are gigantic. There are ships all over the world, not just here.

Some people think the government isn't telling us everything. Some think it's our creations turned against us. Anything is possible.

Some people are convinced that this is the start of the apocalypse. Perhaps it needs to be. For everyone. Maybe it'll bring us peace, or it'll be the end.

They watch. They are there. We are here. We are paranoid.

Some say war. Some say peace. Some say hide. Some say run. I say hope is greater than despair.

We will die to ourselves and suspense before they act.

We will be our worst enemy.

The hope is simple: SURVIVE!

42

History Repeats Itself

Their voices are drowned out by the others. They tried to warn of all that would transpire. Past will always haunt us, but it is better to listen than feign ignorance.

People never look past the surface. Won't listen to any more than what they can see.

Commonly said, rarely listened to:
'History repeats itself.'

Write off school, and we are bound to see history repeat. New players, same story.

They tried to say, but people ignored them.

When nukes fall, the world will cry, but they'll shrug and say 'Well no surprise here'.

The world will burn. If only the people had listened to them.

They yelled and screamed: 'Listen to me!'. But they were drowned out, they were given no heed.

They whisper in the dark. "The world will burn...It is too late."

43

Back to Me

I had lost everyone, so I left. I traveled across the world and met new people. I settled down with my new friends. I had everything again—people I loved, and people that loved me.

I traveled the world and got everything I could want. I was happy—I had it all. I'd look back at what had been and was happy with where I was.

Until...I realized I was all alone again. I had worked so hard to end up right back where I had started.

I had lost everything...AGAIN!

Everyone I loved is gone.

Everything I had, has vanished, right before my eyes.

Deep down I am who I was before...

Did I ever really change?

44

Let Go of Me

"Let me go!" Dani shouted, startling awake. "Just a nightmare. Just a nightmare." She whispered between deep breaths. She pushed herself out of bed to make sure she hadn't woken anyone else up.

"Whoa." She gasped as she nearly collided with Celso with Macie hugging his waist.

"What's wrong?" Macie asked in a hushed voice, grabbing onto Dani instead.

"I had a nightmare. I'm sorry. I didn't mean to wake you." Dani smiled at the little girl. She ran her hand through Macie's raggedly cut hair. "Let's get you back to bed. Come on." Taking Macie's hand she led the smaller girl back to the room she shared with the others.

"What about you?" Macie asked, pouting.

"I'm going to go back to bed too. Sleep well, Little Mouse." Dani turned to leave and saw Celso waiting.

Together they headed up to the roof.

"A nightmare?" Celso asked, looking out at the neon lights of the city.

"Nightmare…" Dani repeated, holding up her mechanical arm in the lights. She glanced up at him as he covered the eye replaced by The Mechanics.

45

Unicorn

Hair as white as snow. Body tall and strong. A horn that glitters and glistens. The magic of life. You are a beautiful creature. Among the green of nature in the beauty of moonlight, I admire your beauty and the grace you bring to life.

Nothing is as gorgeous as you. No one can change that. Even in the light of the sun, your existence is pure.

So when I saw your horn seemed dull and your body lying weakly in the dirt, I didn't know what to do. As blood stained your coat and clashed with nature around you. As the blood pours from a wound far too big to be healed. The sun is setting and pulls at your beauty. You are restless. I wish to lend you my strength, my life, or anything at all.

And even as your life fades from you, your grace is ever present. I still admire you for your beauty and your grace. You are a beautiful unicorn.

You were a beautiful unicorn.

46

Friend of the Dead

Do you know what a Soul Eater is? No? Then let me tell you.

They are more than a monster that consumes souls. So let me tell you the story of the first.

A village had poor harvests year after year, just enough to survive. The people decided the only way to fix their harvest was to sacrifice to the God of Life and Harvest. They chose the sacrifice, a small helpless baby girl. They asked the Gods to grant them what they wished, a bountiful harvest. The God of Harvest didn't want the sacrifice, but blessed them at the cost of breaking equipment. The God of Harvest told the Goddess of Life to do what she wished with the child. The Goddess took the child's soul from where it had drifted and returned it to the child. She then took this small helpless child to the Woman of the Woods, for this woman cared much about life and a true belief in the Goddess. The Goddess would watch over the girl, as she felt it was her own. The child learned to give peace to the lost souls that wandered in the forest and saved the souls that weren't ready for death to take them; just as the Goddess had done for her.

47

The Beasts of Kans Cliff

The beasts of Kans Cliff were the livelihood of many of the people. The people of Kans were the tamers, the beasts protected the people. But one day the beasts no longer walked the cliffs with the people, no one knew where they had gone.

Everything was lost. Not just at Kans Cliff, but at the rivers and the plains. Those that ruled the sky and in the caves, all the beasts had vanished. Only the people were left. The people became a threat to themselves for they would kill, without a reason.

Unlike the beasts, the people did not vanish. They were slain. Blood muddied the dirt and ran through the rivers. Blood seeped into every crack within the land. The stench of death lingered in the air as the corpses rotted and bled. The protectors did not return to their people.

When the last of the blood was spilled, everyone thought that would be the end.

And then—The world burned.

48

The Twins

Alex and Xela were mischievous twins who were always together. One day Xela just seemed to disappear. She was never found, and Alex stopped speaking. He hadn't communicated with anyone since his sister had vanished. It had been ten years since then.

Alex hadn't laughed, cried, or spoken. No one was spared of his silence. No one knew his voice anymore. They were eight when she disappeared. Today he turned eighteen. They turned eighteen. Though he wouldn't talk, every year he would sit and eat cake beside what was her memorial. It had been built by their parents when they lost hope that she would come home. He sits in silence and stares out beyond the edge of the city.

Some people believe he thinks she is still out there, but the forest consumes the lost. She won't come home. She can't.

The people watch him slowly move around town these days. Some try to compel him to speak. Alex always seems to be looking through them.

His parents always say that they haven't truly had either of their children since Xela vanished, though they never said it to

Alex.

Today seemed different.

As the sun began to set, the winds ruffled his hair. He whispered, "She's calling."

49

The Tattered Dress

"I AM FREE!" She screamed to the sky. Her cheaply made dress was tattered and torn. The plush green grass cushioned her feet, bare and scarred, for the first time in years.

In the moonlight she celebrated. The first light she'd seen in years, besides the fire. The fire that had glowed ever so bright as her chains were broken and she ran from the cells where she'd been kept.

The roar of the flames was all that echoed around her. The noise of the people and the machines were silent like they never had been before, but now she was greeted by only her own, existence. Even the fields held no noise to reach her ears.

She was alone and lost. That didn't matter, for she was free, and that was all she'd wanted.

The moon and the stars are the leading light. She could only hope that they would show her the path to take.

Freedom from the chains that burned.

Freedom from the men that taunted.

Freedom at last.

50

Consumed ⋆

The world is all-consuming. The sky remains darkened at most hours. The ground is covered in rubble from buildings and the bones of the dead.

A cat as black as the shadows that would be cast walks among the bones, searching for food in this mostly abandoned world. People seldom wander, and even when they do, the cat would then rather hide.

As the sun sets, the darkened sky is highlighted briefly with reds and oranges. With the sun set the world itself seemed to breathe. Everything began to shift as if the world had awakened. The cat perched on top of a pile of overturned cars that overlooked the animals that now searched the rubble.

On the other side of the road, another cat was perched just the same. Only this cat was white as snow, with piercing blue eyes. The black cat's green eyes stared into the blue eyes of the other. The world gave way for no one. The world crumbled away.

51

Breath of the Dragon

The breath of a dragon is the most powerful in the world, so being the last Dragon leads to being hunted. The humans hunt for the dragon's breath.

I have hidden away in a land long wasted by the power of man. A land where few dare tread, and those that do die long before they reach me. Though I can smell them I will not dare get close to the border where mankind waits and wishes for my breath.

Days become years, and years become decades, and decades become centuries. Slowly they pass, all blurring into one. I have aged.

One day I awaken to the scent of a man at the threshold of my home. I roar out fire, for he is unwelcome here. He calls out, his voice laced with fear and sadness.

"Beast of beauty, beast of might, I bring you a gift." His voice echoes down the halls that man once called home.

I have found the man cowering, I don't want him here.

"Forgive me," He whispers, "I tried to keep it safe, but I failed." He set before me an egg and bows.

My egg. My egg is broken. It was taken many years ago, but man cannot hatch a dragon. This man returned my egg. I breathed and bathed the man and my egg with the last of my dragon's breath.

52

Voices in his Head

The voices in Emros's head had long been whispering. He couldn't remember when they began but knew they would never leave. No matter how far he may run, they would still be there. They called for violence, even in peace. He struggled to ignore these voices whenever they did choose to whisper in his ear. The friends he had could not quell the voices either, for the voices knew something Emros did not, these friends would betray him. Quieter the voices were when beside him stood his only real friend.

Take all life...

Whisper the voices. His hand rests upon the hilt of the sword long sheathed, for he promised himself he would draw no more blood. Before him now his home burns; and the fire licks the sky of the blackened night. The roar of the flames is chased by silence to the break of day. They had come to his home, where he had struggled to remain peaceful. They, these so-called Righteous knights, had come and destroyed his home. His friend, who had helped to keep his voices at bay, now lay slain in the burnt remains of what Emros had called his home.

Take all life...

At his waist, Emros reached for a mask. A mask that he had not worn, as he had sworn to no longer oblige the voices in his head. That was before the knights had chosen to hurt him; before they had broken the chains that held the voices back. Now the voices would rule, and the Crimson Eye would show no mercy. He would see their blood.

TAKE ALL LIFE...

53

Remember the Dreams?

Do you remember your dreams? Yes; well good for you. No; then the Vision Seizer has been in your head.

The Vision Seizer is a creature that visits in the night and steals the dreams you have. It doesn't always visit, so sometimes you may remember, and other days you may forget.

No one knows why the creature exists or what it does with the dreams it collects.

Dreams are strange. Many inexplicable, some enlightening, and plenty missing in the smoke the Vision Seizer leaves behind. No one has seen this creature, so you may never know even if you do. If you could ward off this creature, would you? Or is it a blessing to forget those dreams it takes?

What good is it to remember?

Is forgetting okay?

Why can't we decide?

Though we have all of these questions, we have no answers.

.

54

Hotel of the Resting

"Hello there. How may I help you?" The man dressed in a suit greeted a young lady in simple clothes.

"I-I think I'm lost." She glanced around the large room with silver-gilded decorations. The room went up so high she couldn't see the top, as balconies wrapped around the marking where the floors were located. People rushed about wherever her eyes looked.

"Well then, you have found the right person. I guarantee that if you are lost, you won't be."

"I don't know where I am."

"Oh, that is an easy question to answer. Welcome to the Hotel of the Resting. A place where the souls of the living come to stay once they have passed on."

"Passed on? I'm dead?" She asked, suddenly confused.

"Yes, but this is your home now. If you'd like I'll help you find your room. Otherwise, if you would rather you can watch over those that you had to leave behind." He pointed off to a door labeled *Viewing Area*. People of all ages walked in and out of the room some, crying and others laughing. "I hope you find peace here." He told her as she headed off.

55

We Are Dolls

We sit in a box, some in a house. The giant comes and dresses us up. We tell stories. Some days it is the same story, but sometimes it changes.

We cannot talk. We cannot move. The giant does those things for us. We are not alive, we do not feel. We simply exist.

The giant dresses us in elegant clothes; not all are so lucky. Some get mixed and matched sets, and others may not get any, but at least we are played with.

The ones that sit on top of the shelf, even the giant can't reach. They are never played with. Yes, they are pretty, but it seems so…so lonely. We've traded hands plenty of times. The first giant has grown oh, so big, and so has the second. Now we belong to the third.

The first is there, the third is crying, how did I cause this? The first fixes my hair before setting me on the shelf. The second brings food. I have been forgotten. I am alone with the others. How…sad.

56

The Wind Whispers

"Can you hear the whispers in the wind? As it rushes by, do you hear the words it screams? Voices cry in silent whispers, but will you ignore them? They want your help or so they will wish you dead!" The woman's voice was laced with anger.

"That sounds like a threat." The King spoke.

"Listen to the voices. They are desperate, and you...YOU! You are selfish and pitiful. May the winds be the last to call your name!"

"Take her away." The King motioned for his guards to remove the woman.

"Yes, Your Majesty." They called out, taking the woman away.

The sun set and the moon rose in a clouded sky. The king stood upon his balcony. The wind ruffled the curtains behind him.

Selfish! The word thundered in his ears.

Pitiful! The wind began to howl through the room behind him.

Failure! A whisper in his ear.

The King shall die! The voices cried.

"No!" The King held his head in his hands.

Too late. You should have listened when we wanted to talk. The wind threw him from the balcony out into the garden.

57

At the Dance

During the party, the guests danced in the ballroom. Overly adorned in fancy dresses as the night falls. On every table, the centerpieces are gilded in gold. Men and women entangled in the evenings' dance. Elegant and graceful the dancers move across the floor.

Dinner is served on trays of gold, and the food tastes sweet. The servants bring the guests food as quickly as possible. Hearing their call, the servants rush to serve the masters. Everyone seems to know that their names may be called, yet this dance continues.

Yawning, the people are exhausted, now that the moon has risen high in the sky. Anyone can see that the dance is coming to an end. Ready to rest for the day that will come tomorrow. Even so, the dancers still dance.

58

Naturalia

Naturalia is a beautiful thing.

A building of great stature that fell out of use in time, reclaimed by the beauty of nature. The plants nestle into the crooks and crannies of a place once home to others. Windows that once had curtains of fabric now have curtains of vines and moss. Now the halls are lined with moss and house the critters once unwelcome.

Trees push away and through, soldiers reclaiming land once more for nature.

A home is always a home, regardless of who lives there. Once there may have been the cries of children, but now the calls of birds and chatter of mice fill the air here. And, yes, in the dark it may seem eerie, but the eerie beauty is still just that: beauty.

The world is beautiful! Natural and man-made each has its elegance, yet together they are powerfully vocal of the power She holds. Mother Nature takes back what we no longer seem to want.

Would you walk through the places of abandoned beauty?

59

Escape

"Where did he go?" A man yelled.

"Find that Crawler." Another yelled out.

"It's too dark!" Called another.

"I don't care! Find it!"

Somewhere in the city streets a boy crawled into the back of a wagon and held his breath, as the darkness of the night consumed him. The wagon jerked forward as it moved.

"You there, stop!" A man called.

"No…" The boy whispered, pulling his knees to his chest, where he was branded with the mark of a Crawler.

"What's the problem? I have to get my selling to the capital. I gave notice that I would leave in the night." The driver of the wagon spoke.

"I see. A Crawler escaped. We are looking for it. Have you seen it?" The officer man asked.

"I apologize. Can't say I have. I'd tell you if I did, best of luck in your search."

The wagon lurched forward once more. A few hours passed, and the sun began to rise.

"Come out and eat. I know you're there. You hid well, but you can't get past an old man like me," The wagon man called.

"Why didn't you tell them then? You could get killed." The boy asked, crawling up to the front of the wagon.

"Because. Freedom is beautiful." The old man smiled, pulling up his sleeve to show the boy his arm.

60

A Memory from the Past

I stare at this symbol embossed on the front of the letter. I haven't seen it since I was a kid, *The Order of the Faded Fox,* the emblem of a fox half-gone, that I'd drawn once. My friends and I made a pact that the forest was to be protected. We had 'sealed' the forest in jest, but then my family moved. I never heard anything from my friends either since then.

So how, after all these years, did this find its way to my door? Slowly I open the letter. This has to be a prank, but how?

Dearest Hidden Badger; a name long gone to me, yet an important one once in my past.

We hope this finds you well. Time has passed. I hope, even though this may be a surprise, that you may find time to join us for the Festival of the Forest. Tired Bear, Quiet Wasp, and Lone Snake shall all be in attendance.

I trust you will remember your way and words, till then Hidden Badger.

Your Silent Guardian

Her, but how? She got sick. She is alive, but every record says she's dead. How? Why? Well, I guess, I'll take a trip down memory lane.

61

A Helping Hand ⋆

"Here, I'll help you!" Mika called out cheerfully helping Dimitri move the surfboard off the beach and into the garage.

"Thanks, but I didn't need help, Mika." Dimitri rolled his eyes at Mika.

"Whatever!" Mika punched his friend's shoulder.

"What do you want to do today? We can't be out too late."

"Let's go for a walk."

"Okay. Let's go."

They headed for the cliffs overlooking the beach. They walked along the cliffs and down below the water raged.

"It's beautiful here." Dimitri smiled at Mika. The sun was setting now.

"We have to head back now." Mika smiled up at Dimitri. As Mika turned to head back the way they'd come he froze.

"What's the matter?" Dimitri asked, indifferently from behind Mika's back.

"I can't move…" Mika tried to turn to face his friend.

"Here, I'll help you." Dimitri leaned close and whispered, and pushed Mika over the edge.

62

Who is She? ★

Her gaze is sharp and elegant. Her eyes are blue like the depths of the ocean. Full of order. Blonde hair falls around her face. Dressed in red, she walks through the halls lined with statues and men who bow. She is inherently perfect. No one would dare speak ill of her. She is Sybell Dering.

The woman's eyes were icy cold and her stare hollow and empty. Her presence alone frightened the people who saw her. Her hair is messy and dark as if coated in dirt. Down the hall, she walks servants bowed, and her weapons drawn. Her dress is soaked in blood. She is Sybell Dering.

Her voice carries through the halls. The servants scurry. She is terrifyingly beautiful. Bathed in the moonlight the blood-stained dress seems ill fit, but her confidence makes it all seem okay.

She is Sybell Dering.
The Woman Bathed in Red.

63

Hidden in the Dark

The darkness hides everything. Evil and good, it's all unseen in the dark. The dark is where the monsters hide—those that sleep and those that wander. Lap at the drinks of 'morrow from glasses. Eating food passed through the light. The monsters scream and fight, but we seem to pay them no heed—the beasts and monsters of today, tomorrow, and yesterday.

Some wish them dead, some wish them peace. Monsters are seen as negative, but *what if they weren't?*

Monsters hide in the dark like the monsters under our beds, like in our nightmares. But that's not true, monsters live in every place we exist, in every breath we take.

We are the monsters.

It just so happens that in the dark we choose to bare our teeth and not play pretend.

How can we hunt monsters?
When we are the monsters.

64

Fear the Fire

"What do you want?" Asor asked. He glared through his black hair at the man who sat across from him.

"You need to be more careful." The man said.

"Yeah, yeah. Whatever. Not my problem—"

"Asor. You should be fearful. You are going to get yourself killed!" The man raised his voice a little.

"I'm already dead! I have nothing to fear." Asor stood up from the table, flames seemed to dance in his eyes.

"Asor." The man warned.

"I am not afraid. I am already dead." Asor grabbed the table as purple flames engulfed his hands.

"Learn to be afraid." The man dumped water onto Asor's hands. "Or else you will lose the privilege of doing missions."

"Fear would make me weak," Asor mumbled, wiping his hands on his shirt.

"No, fear makes you alive, Asor. So how about you learn to live? Child of Fire learn to fear." The man stood to leave, patting Asor atop the head.

65

The Castle of Darkness

The Castle of Darkness sits atop a mountain, unreachable. No matter how the sun shines, it is a gloomy place shadowed with darkness.

Tales are told of the castle, but so much time has passed, and no one knows the truth.

The story most often told is that the King who once reigned there was cruel to the gods, so they cursed the king and his home to be untouched by the light. The light was a blessing he didn't deserve. One of the Gods split the land so no soul could reach his gates. So the castle sits seemingly frozen in time.

The crows fly among the shadows, though most question why, after so much time, how there could still be life within those empty walls and halls. The Corvus must simply enjoy the darkness of that castle.

Some wonder if there are still souls that walk the halls. Would souls wander in the dark? Is that part of the curse, or would they be able to rest?

Some days answers seemed to be within reach and others further than the eye could see.

66

Child of Tomorrow

Dear Child of the future,

How I wish I could hear you laugh. Or wipe your tears when you cry. How I wish you would face no turmoil.

Time has moved too fast, and now you must face a world not ready for you either. I hope you won't, but I know the chances are high. You'll see people rip apart the world with every piece of themselves. With words, with weapons, anything that can pierce the skin of the fragility of humanity. Humanity will be torn. I am not sure it will be mended. But for you, dear child, I hope it mends and you may be joyous.

I know not to make a promise. Promises are easily broken. So I'll give you my hope. I hope you will live a happy life in a world with people who listen before speaking and always consider compromise.

So dearest child of the future I give you my hope.

Sincerely the Past

67

Wet Clockwork

Boards reach out into the lake hidden from prying eyes. The boards had been damaged and fragmented over time. Once maybe it was a fishing pier or a place for someone who once docked a boat or where children swam.

Brass admired the broken boards that looked like they could collapse at any second.

"Brass!" A voice called out from behind him.

"Yes, Stitch?" Brass called back, looking over his shoulder at his sister.

"We shouldn't be here. Let's go. Are you trying to get hurt?" Stitch yelled at him.

"Go if you want. I'm just looking! I'm not going out there. I am not stupid."

"You better not get your circuits wet! I won't save you or carry you home, got it?"

"Got it." Brass laughed at his sister.

"One day, I'll walk a dock that is full of mysteries." He said to himself after Stitch had walked away. He stepped onto the wooden board before him on the ground. It splintered beneath him. "This one is far too dangerous."

68

The Man with the Cloak ★

He has haunted me ever since I can remember, the man with the green cloak, in dreams and life. I've stopped talking about it to people, most of them think I am crazy if I do.

I had never considered asking anyone what it could mean, but then I found her listing: Eowyn a medium, someone known to look inside for answers.

"Hello?" I ask as I enter the small shop piled high with items, but no signs of human life.

"Hello! Welcome! I'm Eowyn, you must be Fay!" An older woman appeared, taking my hand and leading me to a new room much cleaner than the rest of the shop.

"Yes," I manage to meekly whisper as I sit across from her at the only table in the room.

"So, what answers can I help you find on this day?" She asked, leaning forward towards me in her chair.

"I keep having these…visions…of a man in a green cloak. I would just like to know what it means." I explain it, suddenly unsure she can help me.

"The Angel of Death. He brings you peace. A guardian. You

should never fear the path you take, for he will protect you."

69

The World Burned ★

The boy got off his horse as someone came up to where he waited. He knew she was coming.

"Don't you know who I am?" The woman grabbed the young boy forcing him to face her.

"Yes. I do." He smiled at her. "I just don't care."

She gritted her teeth. "I am the ruler of this world!"

"Your world is burning." The boy responded, peaking past her at the fires. The fires burned high in the sky above what was a burning city.

"You will respect me!" The woman spared a glance over her shoulder at the city.

"Why do *you* deserve my respect? You are leaving your people to burn. Why should I do anything you say?" The boy released the reins of his horse. The horse fled away from them, as the sound of the fires roared around them.

"Are you crazy?" She shouted, trying to get a hold of the horse and failing.

"Are you?" He asked. The boy climbed up on a rock and turned to watch the fires.

"This land will be consumed by the fire! We have to get out—"

"We? Trying to pull at my heart?" The boy asked, turning to face the woman.

"You'll die if you stay here."

"You think I wish to live? I started the fire. I wouldn't abandon my creation. A leader should stand by their world even as it burns." The boy laughed, basking in the fire that grew closer to them.

70

Can I Help?

A scientist sat working on papers trying to find a solution.

"What if you did—" His creation spoke.

"No." He said.

"But, okay what if you did—"

"No."

"How about—"

"No."

"Just consider if you—"

"NO! No, and no. Please shut up." The scientist turned to look at his creation.

"You know what your problem is? You lack imagination."

"Hardly, I created you didn't I?" The scientist laughed, turning back to the papers on his desk.

"Then why aren't you listening?" The creation asked, standing beside the scientist.

"Fine. What do you want to say?" The scientist asked, leaning back in his chair.

"What if you did fixes to the others? Or find someone who can? They are in pain and I'd like it if they weren't in pain. They would like to be fixed."

"Pain? Do you feel pain?" The scientist turned to look at his creation.

"Yes. Should I not?" The creation asked, looking into the eyes of the scientist.

71

The Buttons

"I'll be right back. Okay, Noé?" Noé's dad said as he headed for the door.

"Yeah, yeah," Noé responded, rolling his eyes and leaning back in the desk chair facing a large screen.

"Don't touch anything!" His dad opened the door and stepped out.

Noé looked at the screen and the controls that were laid out in front of him.

"Why do I have to be here? This is so boring!" Noé groaned.

"Because you are grounded. Mr. Noé." His dad's AI answered.

"I didn't want an answer."

"Oh, but you asked a question?"

"Ugh…shut up, you stupid AI."

"You seem—"

"I said to be quiet, you damn thing!" Noé shouted, standing up and punching the desk in front of him.

An alarm blares and the door lock clicks. Noé rushes over and tries the door, only to find it's locked. He can't open it.

"What just happened? Did I do that?" Noé asked, panicked.

"Answer me!"

"But you said—" The AI started.

"What happened!?" He screamed.

"You hit a button. I don't know what it did. I'm sorry Mr.Noé."

"Noé?" His dad asked from the other side of the door. His voice was faint, "Are you okay?"

72

Don't Say Goodbye

They always say 'Don't say goodbye', just 'See you later', but what about the times you don't get to say anything? No goodbyes, not even a see you later. I've said goodbyes, see you later, and even no words at all. They all hurt, their pains each different.

Goodbye isn't always painful. Sometimes it's just the right word to use, and not every time is the last. But when the goodbyes are the ones that hurt, they hurt a lot. Goodbyes hurt because you know you may never see them, hear them, or speak to them again. Goodbye is a final word to let go of someone.

See you later. A pause, a promise that you'll be together again, even after life and all that has transpired. The hurt comes, because you know you'll be different when you next meet.

No words—a pain caused by trying to figure out what it is that you did wrong, or if you could have made the outcome different. You lost them, and there was nothing to say or do. No words make you dwell on what could have been.

Goodbye or see you later.

DON'T SAY GOODBYE

The choice is yours.

Acknowledgments

Thank you to my beta readers: Grandma, Katelyn, Nick, and Jhenna.

You made it possible for this work to become the best it could be and helped me prepare to share it with the world. Thank you for believing in my dream and for loving my stories. I'm also thankful to each of you for loving the stories I did not have confidence in and reassuring me that they were good.

Thank you to all the readers who may read this.
I hope you will join me in another world sometime.

About the Author

Katherine Myers is an author from Central Minnesota. Katherine loves books that fall into the genres of fantasy, poetry, and short stories. Her first work was published through an online challenge and was a poetry book called *Made in Tomorrow*. She has many stories currently in the works. When not writing, she is busy working and studying.

You can connect with me on:

🌐 https://katherinemyersauthor.wordpress.com

🔗 https://www.instagram.com/katherine_myers_author